W9-AUR-667

DATE		
11-17		
T		
12-17		
10-24		
10-26		
5-17		
10-4		
10-8		
11-7		
11-7		

DISCARDED

BAKER & TAYLOR BOOKS

A NOTE TO PARENTS

When your children are ready to "step into reading," giving them the right books—and lots of them—is as crucial as giving them the right food to eat. **Step into Reading Books** present exciting stories and information reinforced with lively, colorful illustrations that make learning to read fun, satisfying, and worthwhile. They are priced so that acquiring an entire library of them is affordable. And they are beginning readers with an important difference—they're written on four levels.

Step 1 Books, with their very large type and extremely simple vocabulary, have been created for the very youngest readers. **Step 2 Books** are both longer and slightly more difficult. **Step 3 Books,** written to mid-second-grade reading levels, are for the child who has acquired even greater reading skills. **Step 4 Books** offer exciting nonfiction for the increasingly proficient reader.

Children develop at different ages. **Step into Reading Books,** with their four levels of reading, are designed to help children become good—and interested—readers *faster*. The grade levels assigned to the four steps—preschool through grade 1 for Step 1, grades 1 through 3 for Step 2, grades 2 and 3 for Step 3, and grades 2 through 4 for Step 4—are intended only as guides. Some children move through all four steps very rapidly; others climb the steps over a period of several years. These books will help your child "step into reading" in style!

To all the trick or treaters who
scare ME when I see them on Halloween

Library of Congress Cataloging-in-Publication Data:
Prager, Annabelle. The spooky Halloween party / by Annabelle Prager ; illustrated by Tomie de Paola. p. cm. —(Step into reading. A Step 2 book) SUMMARY: Albert doesn't recognize anyone at Nicky's Halloween party, even when they take off their masks. ISBN: 0-394-84961-2 (pbk.); 0-394-94961-7 (lib. bdg.) [1. Halloween—Fiction. 2. Parties—Fiction] I. de Paola, Tomie, ill. II. Title. III. Series. PZ7.P8864Sp 1989 [E]—dc19 88-37571

Manufactured in the United States of America   3 4 5 6 7 8 9 10

STEP INTO READING is a trademark of Random House, Inc.

Step into Reading

The Spooky Halloween Party

By Annabelle Prager
Illustrated by Tomie de Paola

A Step 2 Book

Random House New York

CHAPTER ONE

"<u>Whoo whoo whoo</u>," said Nicky.

"Why are you asking me who?"

  said Albert.

"I'm not asking you who,"

  said Nicky.

"I'm getting ready

  to scare everybody on Halloween."

"What are you doing on Halloween?"

  asked Albert.

"Didn't I tell you?" said Nicky.

"I am going to have

a spooky Halloween party

at my new apartment.

Everybody is going to be scared

out of their wits."

"Like who?" said Albert.

"Like you and Jan,

my cousin Suzanne,

and Morris and Doris and Dan,"

said Nicky.

"Getting scared on Halloween

is for little kids," said Albert.

"Nothing is going to scare me."

They stopped in front of
Nicky's new apartment house.
"What are you going to be
on Halloween?" said Albert.
"I can't tell you," said Nicky.
"Nobody will know who anybody is
till after we go trick or treating.
It will be scarier that way."

"Nobody is going to scare me,"
said Albert.

"I will know who everybody is
right away."

"That's what you think,"
called Nicky
as he headed for his front door.

CHAPTER TWO

Albert went home

to think of a good Halloween costume.

"Nicky thinks he's so smart,"

said Albert.

"But all he has to do

is go <u>whoo</u> <u>whoo</u> <u>whoo</u>

and I will know him right away."

<u>Ring-a-ding-ding,</u> the phone rang.

It was Jan.

"Will you lend me a mop

for Nicky's spooky Halloween party?"

said Jan.

"I have a good idea for a costume.

You will never guess who I am."

"I have a good idea too," said Albert.

"But I haven't got a mop."

Albert hung up.

"I'll bet Jan
   is going to be a witch,"
thought Albert.
"And she thinks that
   witches ride on mops.
   How dumb can she be?"

<u>Ring-a-ding-ding,</u>

the phone rang again.

This time it was Dan.

"Guess what?" said Dan.

"Nicky invited me

to his spooky Halloween party,

and I am going to be a pirate!"

"You are not supposed to tell

what you are going to be,"

said Albert.

"Why not?" asked Dan.

"Because now I will know who you are,"

said Albert.

"But you already know who I am,"

said Dan.

"Oh, Dan," said Albert,

"you never get the point."

Albert hung up.

Albert got out the box of old clothes.

"I am sick of the clothes

in this box," he said.

"I have worn them all before.

I know, this year I will wear the box!

I will be a robot.

Nobody will know it is me.

We will see who is going to scare who

at Nicky's spooky Halloween party."

CHAPTER THREE

On Halloween Albert set out

for Nicky's new apartment house.

He was wearing the box upside down.

All you could see of Albert

were his arms and legs.

He practiced talking

in a squeaky robot voice.

"Where is Nicky's party?"

Albert asked the doorman

at Nicky's new apartment house.

"Take the elevator to the fifth floor.

It is apartment C,"

said the doorman.

Albert got in the elevator.

A princess wearing a gold crown

and a big pair of high heel shoes

got in the elevator too.

She pushed button number five.

"She must be Nicky's cousin Suzanne,"

thought Albert.

"You are not very scary,"

  Albert said to the princess.

"I would rather be pretty,"

  said the princess.

"Are you going

  to the spooky Halloween party

  on the fifth floor?"

"Of course," said Albert.

"Then you can come with me,"

  said the princess,

"so the spooks won't get me."

"Don't be silly,"

  said Albert.

"There aren't any spooks."

The elevator stopped at five.

A clown and a monster

were running up and down the hall.

"Follow me," said the princess.

Albert followed the princess

around a corner.

They stopped at an open door.

"Hey, look at the robot," said a witch.

"Who could it be?"

Albert felt very good.

"I will know them," he thought.

"But they won't know me!"

CHAPTER FOUR

It was really spooky at the party.

The only light came from

three little pumpkins.

Albert looked around for Nicky.

Was he the owl flapping his wings?

Or was Nicky the goblin

with the stocking over his head?

And which witch was Jan?

The one with the broom

or the one with the shopping bag?

"I know," thought Albert.

"The witch with the broom is Jan.

Somebody must have told her

that witches don't ride on mops."

He went up to the witch

and gave her broom a shake.

"Where is your mop?"

said Albert

in his squeaky robot voice.

"Go away or I will bite you,"

said the witch.

"What's the matter with Jan?"

Albert wondered.

He went up to the other witch.

"You better watch out!"

she hissed in a witch's voice.

"The terrible spooks have cast a spell

on everyone here!"

"They HAVE NOT!" said Albert.

"Wait and see," hissed the witch.

Albert went looking for Dan.

But there were

no little pirates anywhere.

Albert felt a tap on his box.

"It's me," said the princess.

"And I'm scared."

"I'M NOT," said Albert.

Just then the goblin shouted,

"Okay, you guys.

Time to trick-or-treat.

Head for the stairs."

"That goblin sounds bossy,"

thought Albert, "just like Nicky.

And he thought he could fool me."

CHAPTER FIVE

Everybody headed for the stairs.

Albert tried to keep up

with the goblin

and the owl,

but it was hard to run

wearing a box.

And the princess kept losing

her high heel shoes.

So Albert and the princess

had to ring doorbells together.

By the time they reached

the bottom floor,

their bags were heavy with treats.

Then Albert and the princess

climbed back up

the long, lonely stairs.

Black shadows waited at every turn.

Way above them a door went BANG!

"Whoo whoo whoo!"

went a faraway voice.

"Help, a spook!"

yelled the princess.

She grabbed Albert so hard,

he almost fell down the stairs.

"That is not a spook!

It's Nicky!" cried Albert.

"Now I know Nicky is the owl.

That is why he keeps hooting!"

"You don't know anything,"

 said the princess.

"Even I know who the owl is."

 Suddenly a shiver went down Albert.

"Why don't I know who anybody is?"

 he thought.

"Maybe I <u>am</u> under a spell."

 The princess started to scream.

"It's Halloween

 and the spooks

 are going to get us!"

 she yelled.

"Let's get out of here!"

"You said it!" Albert yelled back.

CHAPTER SIX

When Albert and the princess

got back to the party,

Albert's heart was going

thump, thump! thump, thump!

Everybody was waiting in the dark.

"Take off your masks,"

said the bossy goblin.

"I will turn on the lights."

Albert felt better.

Now he would see his friends.

He looked around for Nicky.

The owl was holding

his mask in his hand.

The owl was not Nicky.

The goblin pulled

the stocking off his head.

The goblin was not Nicky either.

And who were the witches?

Albert had never seen

either of them before.

In fact, Albert had never seen

anybody at the party before.

Everyone stared at him.

His heart started to thump again.

His knees began to shake.

"There really are spooks," said Albert.

"Spooks have changed my friends
into strangers!"

CHAPTER SEVEN

Just then the doorbell rang.

"Whoo whoo whoo," went a voice.

"Trick or treat!"

The doorway was full of people.

One was a little pirate.

One was a clown

with hair that looked like a mop,

and one was a ghost with a light

that went on and off.

"Whoo whoo whoo," said the ghost.

"Whoooo can I scare?"

"Look, there is Albert!"

shouted the little pirate.

"Hey, Albert, why didn't you come

to Nicky's Halloween party?"

Albert was all mixed up.

"I <u>am</u> at Nicky's Halloween party,"

he said.

"Aren't I?"

"No, you are at my Halloween party,"

said the goblin.

"This is apartment B.

Nicky lives around the corner

in apartment C."

"So there aren't any spooks after all,"

said Albert.

"I am just at the wrong party!"

CHAPTER EIGHT

"Now you have to come

to the right party,"

said the ghost

in Nicky's bossy voice.

"Everybody has to come to my party.

I've got popcorn to eat

and lots of spooky games to play."

So the right party

and the wrong party

ended in a double Halloween party

at Nicky's house in apartment C.

They played Nicky's spooky games

and screamed and yelled

until their throats were sore.

Finally it was time to go home.

"This was a super-special Halloween
even though it was so scary,"
said the princess.

"You are wrong,"

said Nicky.

"This was a super-special Halloween

just because it was so scary."

And everyone agreed—

even Albert.